SILVER SPURS

story by: Robert Knigge

pictures by: Sally King Brewer

Library of Congress catalog card number 75-10111
I S B N 0-915614-01-4

PRINTED IN THE U.S.A.
Published by
K N O L L W O O D   P U B L I S H I N G
625 Knollwood Drive
WILLMAR, MINN. 56201

HAVE you ever wondered how Santa Claus comes down your chimney to leave all those nice gifts and toys? Well—wonder no more but gather around, for I have a story to tell.

You see, a long time ago everyone had a fireplace to keep them warm and to cook their food. And every fireplace had a chimney.

Once a year at Christmas, Santa came down those large chimneys with treats and toys for girls and boys in many lands.

But then came a change in the times when most people built their homes without fireplaces and large chimneys. This made that large chimney

get smaller

and smaller,

and sometimes,

there
was
no
chimney
at
all!!

Now this made Santa very worried and sad. How could he take gifts and toys to all the little girls and boys if they didn't have a large chimney for Santa to come down?

Just last year Santa got stuck in a red brick chimney that was too small. Santa grunted and wiggled, and wiggled and grunted, but couldn't get out. Santa's reindeer came to help him.

They pulled and tugged . . . and tugged and pulled, and got him free at last. But much time was lost, and part of the seat of Santa's pants! Santa was having so much trouble with those small chimneys.

Everyone knows that Santa has reindeer and
everyone knows that Santa has elves.

But not everyone knows that this biggest problem of Santa's was solved by his smallest elf, Silver Spurs.

Silver Spurs was so small that when the mama doll didn't say, "Ma Ma" after it was all put together, he could slip in between the seams and fix it. But Santa's other elves did their job so well, Silver Spurs had little to do.

The other elves wouldn't let Silver Spurs help make the toys. They thought he was too small and would only get in their way. Sometimes Silver Spurs would look at the toys the elves made and try to find something wrong. And when he couldn't, this made the other elves laugh with glee. Then again he would amuse the other elves by flying very fast in a tight circle, giving the impression of a bright flying saucer.

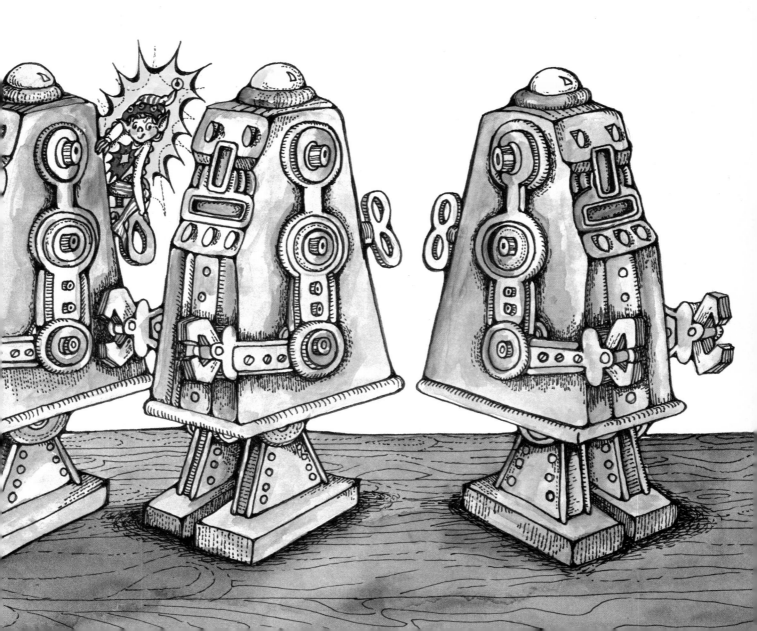

All this made Silver Spurs very tired and he often curled up in a cozy spot to take a long nap. The elves only woke Silver Spurs when they had a special job. Silver Spurs had a bright star on the front of his shirt and had bells up one sleeve of his shirt and down the other. The bright glow of the star and the tinkling bells made it easy for the other elves to find him. Sometimes to wake him, they had to sprinkle him with water. Then like a streak of silver, (for he was as fast as a hoof on Santa's reindeer), he fixed the toys so that once again he could sleep.

Silver Spurs was also one of Santa's smartest elves. He seemed to learn as he slept. Even as people went from fireplaces with large chimneys to cookstoves and furnaces, Santa and his elves went from mama dolls to dancing dolls, and from cast iron wagons to cars with sealed-in motors. It always made Silver Spurs very happy when he could help Santa and the other elves.

Now Silver Spurs loved to snuggle in Santa's soft beard and take his nap. Sometimes when Santa laughed, if you had been there and listened, you might have heard the little bells tinkle and Silver Spurs chuckle, too.

On the day before Christmas, Santa was sitting in his big chair and Silver Spurs was napping in Santa's soft beard. Santa was thinking about the narrow chimneys. The more he thought, the more sad Santa became, and then a tear rolled down his cheek and into his beard — and out jumped Silver Spurs! After Silver Spurs wiped his eyes with the back of his hands, he noticed Santa's long, sad face and asked, ''Why, Santa, what is the matter?''

Santa brushed another tear from his eye and said sadly, "You remember last year when some of the children got their toys late and one little girl didn't get her sewing kit because it was needed to mend the pants I tore? I don't know what we're going to do about those narrow chimneys."

Seeing how sad Santa felt, Silver Spurs shook his little bells, sat down on Santa's finger and thought and thought. Then, with a twinkle in his eye, he jumped up and cried "Santa, I have the answer! Why not take me along to slip down those skinny chimneys or flip through the key-holes in the doors? Then I could open the door and let you in!"

When Santa heard this, he raised his eyebrows and with a big smile he said loudly, "That's it, Silver Spurs! That's it! Let's be on our way! The toys are ready and the children are waiting!" And off they went to deliver the many toys for the little girls and boys.

So if you live in a house without a large chimney, or with no chimney at all, and have wondered how Santa got in to your living room on Christmas Eve, you've got to know that Silver Spurs, the smallest of the elves, was there. And on Christmas Eve, if you see what you might think is a falling star, just wave your hand and shout a cheery "Hi there, Silver Spurs! Merry Christmas!"

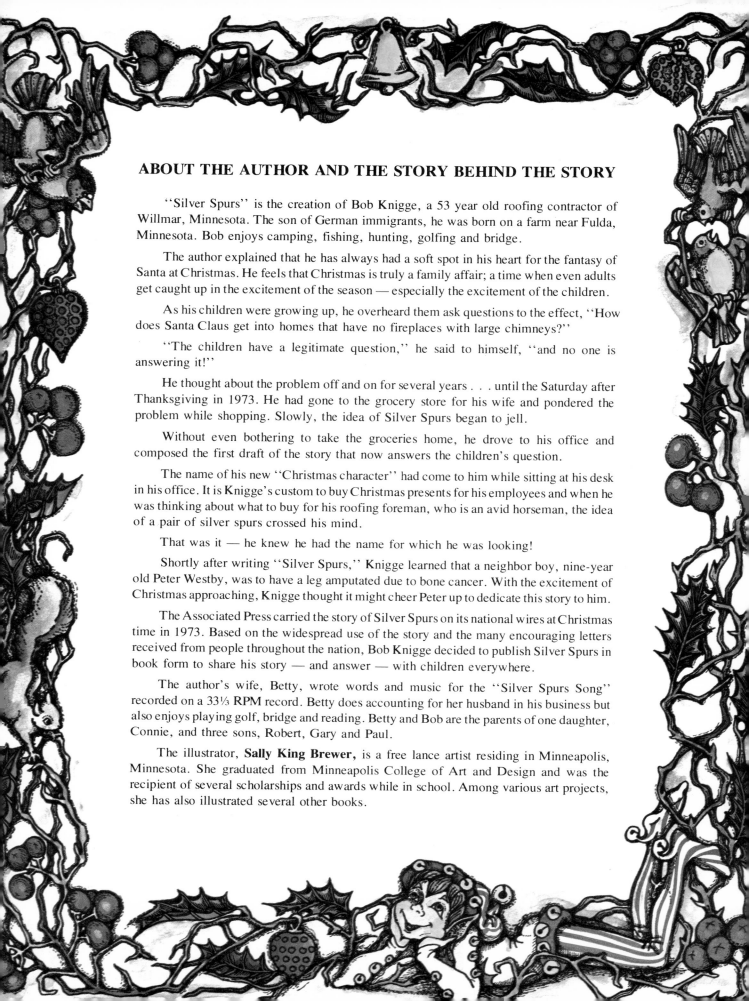

ABOUT THE AUTHOR AND THE STORY BEHIND THE STORY

"Silver Spurs" is the creation of Bob Knigge, a 53 year old roofing contractor of Willmar, Minnesota. The son of German immigrants, he was born on a farm near Fulda, Minnesota. Bob enjoys camping, fishing, hunting, golfing and bridge.

The author explained that he has always had a soft spot in his heart for the fantasy of Santa at Christmas. He feels that Christmas is truly a family affair; a time when even adults get caught up in the excitement of the season — especially the excitement of the children.

As his children were growing up, he overheard them ask questions to the effect, "How does Santa Claus get into homes that have no fireplaces with large chimneys?"

"The children have a legitimate question," he said to himself, "and no one is answering it!"

He thought about the problem off and on for several years . . . until the Saturday after Thanksgiving in 1973. He had gone to the grocery store for his wife and pondered the problem while shopping. Slowly, the idea of Silver Spurs began to jell.

Without even bothering to take the groceries home, he drove to his office and composed the first draft of the story that now answers the children's question.

The name of his new "Christmas character" had come to him while sitting at his desk in his office. It is Knigge's custom to buy Christmas presents for his employees and when he was thinking about what to buy for his roofing foreman, who is an avid horseman, the idea of a pair of silver spurs crossed his mind.

That was it — he knew he had the name for which he was looking!

Shortly after writing "Silver Spurs," Knigge learned that a neighbor boy, nine-year old Peter Westby, was to have a leg amputated due to bone cancer. With the excitement of Christmas approaching, Knigge thought it might cheer Peter up to dedicate this story to him.

The Associated Press carried the story of Silver Spurs on its national wires at Christmas time in 1973. Based on the widespread use of the story and the many encouraging letters received from people throughout the nation, Bob Knigge decided to publish Silver Spurs in book form to share his story — and answer — with children everywhere.

The author's wife, Betty, wrote words and music for the "Silver Spurs Song" recorded on a 33⅓ RPM record. Betty does accounting for her husband in his business but also enjoys playing golf, bridge and reading. Betty and Bob are the parents of one daughter, Connie, and three sons, Robert, Gary and Paul.

The illustrator, **Sally King Brewer,** is a free lance artist residing in Minneapolis, Minnesota. She graduated from Minneapolis College of Art and Design and was the recipient of several scholarships and awards while in school. Among various art projects, she has also illustrated several other books.